LOSING WEIGHT IN GRANNY'S KITCHEN

Ikechukwu Frederick Nwaulu

Publishing partner: Paragon Publishing, Rothersthorpe

ISBN 978-1-78222-820-2

Book design, layout and production management by Into Print
www.intoprint.net

+44 (0)1604 832149

Yesterday is Gone

Yesterday is gone with her many woes;
forget about the darkest shadows
and all the pains and bitterness,
let your mind be on tomorrow's greatness.

Yesterday is gone with her many sorrows;
forget about the nagging worries that arose,
and all the failures and trials of history,
let your mind be on tomorrow's victory.

Yesterday is gone with her futilities;
forget about the gross absurdities
and all the brawling, ranting, raving
let your mind be on tomorrow's saving.

Yesterday is gone with her aches and pains
Forget about the strikes and strains
and all the bizarre things not worth the wait,
let your mind be on tomorrow's faith.

Ikechukwu Frederick Nwaulu
from *Poetic Mirror*

Chapter One

The snow in the mountains was melting and the birds were hibernating. If I had known that I was about to meet the guy who would 'pummel my diet' like a boxer and reconfigure my stature, I would have retraced my steps.

Paul had been longing to have his cousin Mark spend the holiday with him but on each planned occasion a big wall kept rearing its ugly head to foil the plan. It felt as if it was jinxed. It therefore came as a surprise when his cousin called to say he would be coming in five days time to spend the holiday with him.

"The jinx is finally broken!" Paul announced excitedly.

Paul was over the moon about his cousin's visit. He immediately swung into action by getting the visitor's room tidied. His parents were amazed to see the level of effort he put into cleaning the visitor's room. Only last week his mother had asked him to tidy up the sitting room and he did it haphazardly. The way he had tidied the sitting room the previous week was as if someone had rummaged through the room and hurriedly put back all the stuff to avoid being spotted. This angered his mum and she did not pretend to conceal her anger.

While his mum persisted in going on and on about it, Paul's elder sister, Joyce, came to his rescue.

She took her time and tidied up the sitting room and also emptied the rubbish.

This had been the umpteenth time Paul had done such shoddy work. It was therefore both shocking *and* amazing to see him now taking time to hoover and clean the visitor's room so conscienciously in preparation to welcome his *'august visitor'*.

"Paul..." his mum called out from the sitting room.

Paul hesitated a moment before answering his mum.

"Yes Mum," came the response.

"Are you still cleaning the visitor's room?" his mum enquired. "You have spent the last two hours or so cleaning the room."

"I just want to make sure the place is tidy and amenable to Mark," Paul explained.

His mum stood up and went to have a look at what he had been doing.

"Wow!" his mum exclaimed. "This room is *spotless*. So, you have a knack for cleaning rooms ... but you do not apply such dexterity when asked to tidy the sitting room?"

Chapter Two

Paul paused momentarily and stared into space as if expecting to see something. He ignored the question and continued cleaning.

"That is enough Paul; can you go and help your dad in the garden?"

Paul's countenance became gloomy and he feigned ignorance.

"Can you go and help your dad in the garden?" came his mum's voice again. This time she had raised her voice to make sure he heard her well.

Paul dragged his feet and reluctantly walked towards the garden where his dad was busy tilling the soil to transfer the plants from the nursery.

Paul stood at a corner watching his dad with hands akimbo.

"Are you going to help me or not?" came a hoarse voice.

Paul took a cautious step towards his dad and then began to help out. Together they transferred all the plants in the nursery stage.

Paul broke the silence.

"Dad... is Mark still coming to visit us this weekend?"

"I suppose he will. If anything changes, he will let us know." The dad considered for a moment. *"But wait a minute!"* he exclaimed. "The last time Mark visited when I was away, your mum told me you behaved strangely and wouldn't listen to her. I remember asking you about it when I came back and you assured me it would not happen again. But I am beginning to have a feeling that Mark's presence might influence you negatively. In view of that, I will tell him not to visit since I will be away this weekend on a business trip."

On hearing this, Paul moaned and threatened to go to his cousin's house if Mark was not allowed to visit that weekend.

Later, his mum and dad called him to the lounge and spoke to him at length on why Mark wasn't able to visit in the absence of his dad. But all the preaching and hullaballoo fell on deaf ears as Paul said they had already planned to attend a friend's birthday party together over the weekend.

Seeing that Paul was bent on having his cousin that weekend, his father promised to get him a mountain bike when he came back. Originally the bike was supposed to have been for Paul's 16th birthday which was in two months time.

"Yeah!" Paul exclaimed, his eyes shining and looking as if they were about to pop out of their sockets. *"Really?"* he asked. "OK, I will wait till next week, as long as you keep your promise."

"Of course I will. I do not promise and fail."

His father and his mum stood up to retire to their room and told Paul they would call Mark's parents to tell them to reschedule Mark's visit to the following week.

Chapter Three

Young men and women were drinking and dancing away their lives in such a manner one might wonder if it was a race to see who would first 'breast the tape'. In the furthermost corner of the room sat Mark and Paul drinking and chatting hilariously.

"How did you say you managed to get out of your locked house, Paul?" asked Mark.

"Like I told you, my dad promised to buy me a bike if I did not attend the party with you. I agreed but was still thinking of a way to attend the party when you gave me a call to tell me how *you* managed to leave your room unnoticed. I followed suit but it almost turned sour when my dad came upstairs to use the toilet. I almost bumped into him but I quickly hid by the corner and he went past me to his room.

When I saw that he had gone to bed, I removed my shoes and tip-toed to the back door and quietly unlocked it and shut it behind me as quietly as I could ... and off I went," he said, "feeling brave and smart."

While Paul was narrating his strategy, Mark listened with rapt attention as if he was an examiner taking note of his flaws and successes.

"That's brilliant," Mark commended him. "Come on, let us join the other guys on the dance floor."

The duo stood up and danced vigorously to the different tunes. Midway into the party, Mark introduced Paul to smoking.

They both went outside and smoked like chimneys. While they were smoking, Andy the birthday boy joined them and they got chatting.

"Boy!" Paul exclaimed, "I really enjoyed the delicacies you served us.

It was Andy's 18th birthday and he was over

the moon about it and so had invited a full house. The party had started at about 6 o'clock and ended in the wee hours of the following morning.

After the party, at about 3 o'clock, Mark and Paul set off to their different destinations.

When Paul got home, he took off his shoes and tip-toed to his room.

Since Paul's room was opposite the toilet, sometimes his dad would take a cursory look in his room on his way to the toilet just to make sure Paul was alright.

Before Paul left, he had envisaged his dad looking into his room as usual while on his way to the toilet. With that in mind, Paul had put three pillows adjacent to one another on his bed and then covered them with a bed sheet to 'pull a fast one' on his dad.

However, before Paul got back, his dad had called to him to ask him something.

When the 'body' on the bed that was supposed to be Paul remained motionless, Paul's dad had gone and shaken it and quickly uncovered it. He was shocked to find out he had been fooled. He thought of what he should do to get Paul back and an idea came to him. He then removed the pillows and lay on the bed and covered himself exactly the way the pillows had been covered by his son.

When Paul sneaked in after the party in the wee hours of the morning, he uncovered the bed sheet only to find his dad lying on his bed. This really made him jump.

"Do not be scared," his father giggled. "I am not a ghost, I am only 'paying you back in your own coin'.

Chapter Four

"**N**ow that the 'game is up', you no longer qualify to earn yourself a present. And for disobeying me, no more visits from Mark."

As his dad stood up to make for the door, one could tell that he was really furious judging from his enraged countenance. Paul was completely flabbergasted and rattled. His jaw dropped to the floor. He opened his mouth to try to say something before his father left but couldn't find the right word to utter.

As his father left the room Paul was left with mouth agape and staring into space in utter disbelief at the show his father had put on. Paul sat on his bed thinking of what steps he could take next. He put a call across to Mark and related the whole scenario that had just transpired.

Mark laughed raucously over the incident until he could laugh no longer. This got Paul irritated and he threatened to bang the phone down on him if he didn't have anything reasonable to say.

"Wait a minute," Mark said, still giggling and trying to control his laughter, "you have taken the sleep out of my eyes, now on a serious note – don't give a shit! Just continue with your business and at some point they will get fed up with you and let you be."

"But that could attract the anger of my parents," Paul protested.

"That is the idea," Mark replied. "When your parents get annoyed and you stick to your guns, they will later retrace their steps and dance to your tune. If they blow hot, equally blow hot ... tell them you will abscond. I promise you, at the mention of that word all doors will be flung open for you."

As Paul tried to protest further, Mark quickly interjected.

"... Do it mate if you do not want to be messed about with. Goodbye." He dropped the phone and went back to bed.

During the wee hours of that morning, Paul couldn't sleep; he kept on thinking about what Mark had said. He couldn't come to terms with the fact that he should put up such a crude strategy to escape the impending punishment of his dad. Much as he tried to come up with another idea, nothing was forthcoming. In the end, he simply decided he was going to tender his unreserved apology to his dad – and if *that* didn't work, he would continue to implore them by hook or by crook to escape their wrath.

Chapter Five

The next day, Paul walked up to his dad and apologised profusely to him for what had transpired the previous day. His dad shook his head to show his disbelief. However, his dad accepted his apology and made him promise it was not going to happen again.

Paul was over the moon that his dad had not only forgiven him, but that he would still buy him his choice bike on his birthday (although he would have had it before his birthday if he had conducted himself well).

As he was savouring the thought of having a bike soon, a call came in. He picked up his mobile and found out it was Andy, the guy who had recently celebrated his birthday which he had attended.

"Can you please make time for us to catch

up? Let me know if you can come tomorrow evening. I have got something good for you. Let's meet at MacDonald's."

"You want us to catch up tomorrow?"

"Yes," Andy said, "at 5 o'clock."

"OK, I will see you tomorrow," Paul replied, albeit somewhat surprised considering the fact that he was not Andy's bosom pal. He wondered what Andy wanted to see him for.

His meeting with Andy the following day marked a turning point in his life.

When Paul arrived at their meeting point, Andy gestured him to a seat and bought him a burger.

They munched their burgers and other Mac-Donald's delights while still chatting. Andy told him that Mark had related his ordeal to him and he thought he could help him out. Andy tried to make him feel he was a big boy who should not be pushed around. He told him how he had been subjected to similar treatment two years ago – like one incarcerated before he got himself liberated. He also encouraged Paul not to baulk when being told off by his parents. All the advice however fell on deaf ears as Paul couldn't muster enough courage to challenge his parents.

*

A week before Easter and one of Andy's friends invited him to a birthday party. He extended the invitation to Mark. Paul had no problems in attending as it had been organised for during the day.

They ate and drank to their satisfaction. When Paul got home, the smell of alcohol and cigarettes enveloped the room. His dad was so cross with him that he almost smacked him. But Paul was not remorseful as he kept staring into space as his dad was telling him off.

Chapter Six

In a bid to punish Paul for smoking and drinking heavily, his dad stopped giving him pocket money. As Paul was used to getting pocket money from his dad, he could not stand the deprivation of it.

Eventually, Paul contacted Tony, one of the friends he had made at one of the parties. Tony linked him up to a job and after a while Paul moved out of his parents' house and started living with Tony in a one room apartment.

He started living a carefree lifestyle. He ate a lot of junk food as well as processed food, so much so that after five months (when both his parents decided to forgive him) they could hardly recognise him when he went back home. Paul had put on a considerable amount of weight.

Paul had become addicted to eating junk food. By the time eight months had passed, he had become so obese that his parents feared the worst. His love for fast food even surpassed that of Andy whom he picked it up from.

Paul started by eating junk food on Fridays, after which he ate it all the time. Even after eating the food cooked at home by his mum, he still craved junk food.

One day, his mum called him and sat him down in the lounge.

"Paul," his mum called.

"Yes, Mum," he answered.

She cleared her throat:

"My son, as you know your dad is not coming back for two weeks. And when he *does* come back, he will spend another two weeks on some other official assignment. What it means is that you and I will literally be staying on our own for at least two to three weeks without your dad."

"Mum, but Dad did intimate his work itinerary to me."

"Yes… I know he did," his mum responded. "I am only jogging your memory because you have refused to listen to me about changing your diet. Do you at all look at yourself in the mirror? Look at how you have put on so much weight. I will not bear the burden of the health implications associated with obesity if something happens to you."

"I will be fine, don't worry. *Nothing* is going to happen to me," came the response of Paul.

"You have a variety of cooked organic food, I wonder why you always choose to eat a little and reserve the better part of your appetite for junk food."

"I can't help it Mum."

*

His father came back and was equally worried about his son's excessive weight. Paul was, however, unperturbed as he went about his usual business – as if it was the wall being spoken to.

"Do you know that you are becoming *obese* Paul?" his dad warned him, but Paul ignored him.

"This makes you very susceptible to a whole range of health problems," his father warned.

His warnings fell on deaf ears as Paul continued to savour his junk food. He assuaged his appetite week in week out courtesy of the little saving he had accrued working whilst living with Tony, as well as from his pocket money.

This pattern continued until he gained admission into university to study engineering.

*

In the course of attending university, it dawned on Paul that he had all the while been 'fetching firewood infested with ants' which resulted in 'inviting the lizard to a feast'.

As time went on, Paul began to experience low self esteem and he became withdrawn. He felt his course mates always wore a funny look whenever they looked in his direction. This really made him uncomfortable and it got him thinking about what he could do to salvage the situation.

Chapter Seven

One day, when Paul came back home from the university, he was looking moody and disenchanted, and his voice sounded low. This really got his parents alarmed.

"What is the problem Paul?" his mum asked.

"Nothing..." came the faint response of Paul.

"Do not tell me that Paul," his father replied. "Come on, spill the beans. We are your parents, we will *always* be there for you – come rain or shine. It is only a fool who lives near the river bank and still washes his hands with spittle."

"Dad... since I started at university, those I come into contact with seem to resent me, probably because of my weight. Worse still is the opposite sex."

Paul looked really downcast.

"Do not fret," came the reassuring words of

his mum. "But come to think of it, what makes you feel it is because of your weight? Or more to the point, are you sure it is not something playing on *your* mind?"

"It is not mum, I am old enough to interpret the look on someone's face while discussing with them. It is called *psychology*. And I can tell vividly when I see it."

"Hmm..." Paul's mum breathes heavily. "So what are you going to do?"

Before Paul could respond, his dad quickly chipped in.

"Thank goodness you now realise your weight *is* an issue ... and I'm telling you that this is the beginning of your healing process."

"What do you mean, Dad?" Paul enquired.

"Hitherto you felt it was not an issue. You actually felt we were intruding into your privacy, now you know better."

"I see what you mean, Dad. I guess I was a

bit naïve and overwhelmed by my new found craving for junk food. Right, now I have made up my mind to renounce eating junk food, I will devise a strategy to help me achieve my desired weight in eight to ten months," Paul informed his dad resolutely. "At the moment," he continued, "I weigh about 105kg which is equivalent to 16½ stones. My target should be to reduce to about 70-80kg."

"WOW!" the mum exclaimed. "That would really be perfect. That is in no way going to be child's play."

"It sounds daunting but nonetheless achievable," the dad chipped in.

"Dad, Mum..." Paul looked in the direction of his parents with a shining countenance like someone who had eventually found a long lost old friend out of the blue. "I am now determined more than ever to discipline myself to hit the target."

The enraptured expression on his parents' faces showed how impressed they were by Paul's strong desire to shed weight.

"Tell us," his dad said excitedly, "how do you intend to achieve this no mean feat?"

"I would rather not let the cat out of the bag just now," Paul replied. "But definitely I have something in my head which hopefully will do the magic."

"That's OK," replied his dad. "As long as what you do makes you happy and produces a positive result. Just follow your mind and your instinct; I guess you will be fine."

"Thank you, Dad and Mum. Good night," Paul said in appreciation as they all retired to bed.

Chapter Eight

Paul went back to the university and in his hostel in the corner of his room lay a book where he wrote what he ate every day. He started by replacing all junk foods in his diet with cooked meals; he also made a habit of adding vegetables to all his meals. He made sure all the foods with preservatives in his drawer were thrown away and he recorded what he ate on a daily basis as well as weighing himself every week.

After three weeks of sticking to cereal, wholemeal bread, vegetables, pasta, fruits and jacket potatoes, there was no result to show for it. He then added 'wild dancing' to his list as he did not have the time to go to the gym.

When Paul went shopping, he bought a couple of trousers in a size smaller than he wore and hung them in a conspicuous corner in his wardrobe.

One day his friend Andy visited and saw him sweating and breathing heavily.

"What have you been doing mate?" Andy inquired.

"I have been doing a vigorous dance, dancing to this old school tune," came the quick response. "It is one of my sundry strategies to lose weight.

"Hmm.... that sounds interesting," Andy chipped in. "So how often do you do this?"

"Every day for at least thirty minutes to an hour, depending on my mood and the time available."

"And what are all those new trousers doing hanging there?" Andy pointed in the direction where the trousers were hanging. Before Paul could respond he continued, "Are you travelling or did you get them for someone? Of course they look too small for you so they cannot be yours."

"Neither," Paul replied. "Rather, they are what I will be wearing in the next eight to ten months time."

"YOOUUU?" Andy asked sarcastically. "You must be out of your mind. Are you aware that these trousers are size 34-36 and your size is 44? How on earth do you intend to do that?"

"Simply by being consistent with my new found routine. Mind you I do not eat after 6 o'clock in the evening, irrespective of the circumstances, be it birthday party, wedding and the like. I have really disciplined myself and by the grace of God come eight to ten months time I *will* be wearing size 34-36."

"That is great! I like your faith and optimism," Andy commented before taking his leave.

Chapter Nine

till at the university, Paul kept up with his routine as well as his diet. Every three weeks he tried on the small trousers he had bought. He did this for more than ten months and eventually, in the eleventh month, the trousers which were size 34 fitted him. Paul was over the moon. He travelled home and happily announced to his parents how the small trousers which he had bought almost a year ago now fitted him.

"Look at you!" exclaimed his mum. "You have *really* lost weight. It is good for you, try and keep it up," his mum encouraged him.

"Son..." his dad called out. "You backed up your words with action. That's brilliant, and you were really optimistic it was going to work. Optimism without work is dead. You really had

the right frame of mind and that did the magic. Well done. At least you have succeeded in promoting your health. As I always say, *prevention is better than cure.*"

"Thanks dad, my routine continues. I really need to see Andy the *doubting Thomas* now. He laughed at me to scorn when he saw the trousers I had bought. He called me a joker and stuff like that. I bet he will be shocked to see me wearing these trousers."

Later in the evening, Paul went to Andy's house. Andy was really shocked and speechless to see Paul really trimmed down.

"How did you do it? You look great with your new physique. Please just maintain your weight."

Paul kept on smiling and really felt proud of himself. They both drank and had an enjoyable time chatting about life in general.

*

Back in the university, Paul was the toast of the school. Friends and foes alike kept besieging him to share the strategy he had adopted.

Paul simply said:

"Just have the right mindset and the doors will be flung wide open for you."

They kept asking him for details but he simply replied: *"Just have the right frame of mind and always be optimistic.'*

*

Paul remained the same size until he graduated from university. After graduation, he intended to set up a charity organisation to help those who are obese. With the support of his friends, it was soon up and running, offering advice and counselling to lots of people in need of remedy to reduce weight.

His contributions were soon recognised by an international organisation and he was soon working for the World Health Organisation.

His parents were exceptionally proud of him, as too were his sister and friends. They all encouraged him to keep the fire burning.

However, in a cruel twist of fate, one of the women he had helped to lose weight brought charges against him.

*

The lady was called Eunice and she accused Paul of having sexually assaulted her in the course of counselling her. She involved the police and an investigation began in earnest.

Eunice brought one of his favourite T-shirts with an inscription of '*keep fit*' on it and told the police how Paul had wanted to rape her and that she had held him by his shirt. For fear of being seen by people, Paul had taken off his T-shirt and had run away leaving her with the T-shirt.

Paul protested, insisting it had been the other way round. However, he was told his story lacked credibility and he was incarcerated.

This episode in Paul's life really brought grief and sorrow to his family and friends. All efforts made by friends and family to get him released proved futile.

Chapter Ten

While in prison, Paul met a couple of people, one of whom really struck a chord.

James, a middle-aged man became a close friend and Paul told him the circumstances that surrounded his arrest and imprisonment. James told Paul of how his sister had tried all strategies to lose weight without success. Paul shared the strategy he used to lose weight with him. James was really impressed and told him how appreciative he was for the tips. James, however, had almost served his sentence and was to be released in three days time.

After his release, James shared all the tips with his sister and encouraged her to take the diet seriously. In a space of eight months his sister had lost about 25kg. Her weight had gone from 95kg to 70kg.

She was really overjoyed and asked to see the man who had given James those powerful tips. James told her he was not sure if Paul was still in prison. At the insistence of James's sister, they went to the prison where James had first met Paul in search of him.

Fortunately, they found Paul there. James's sister thanked him profusely for the tips; she told him how his tips had boosted her confidence.

Paul acknowledged her gratitude and joked: "You only find something close to this diet in Granny's kitchen" and she chuckled and then continued, "So, what brought you to prison?"

Paul told her how a lady known as Eunice tried to seduce him after he had been counselling her on how to lose weight. He had resisted her and she had grabbed him by his T-shirt. He had removed it and left it with her and then run away. She had then used the T-shirt to set him up, Paul concluded.

James's sister was really furious and she resolved to escalate the case herself.

It transpired that James's sister Glory was a lawyer and their dad was also a lawyer of high repute. She indicated to her dad how Paul had been set up. Her father, already impressed by her new shape (courtesy of the tips given to her by Paul through James while in the prison), promised to deal with the issue.

Her father contacted his colleagues and with a reasonable and concrete defence put up, Paul was eventually released.

Paul was extremely appreciative of their contribution towards his release. Glory told him that it was she who was the one to thank him for saving a *hitherto battered and discouraged life*.

Fate had brought Paul and Glory together. Over time they became the best of friends and along the line a relationship ensued. The relationship continued to develop until it reached a point where it became obvious that the two of them were inseparable.

Glory and Paul eventually tied the knot.

Before they did so, however, Eunice finally confessed to framing Paul and asked for his forgiveness. He forgave her but she was arrested and put behind bars for false accusation.

The charity picked up from where it had stopped, and with the support of his wife, Paul made giant strides and blessed a thousand and one lives.

ABOUT THE AUTHOR

Ikechukwu Frederick Nwaulu studied Mass communication at Federal Polytechnic Oko, Anambra state, Nigeria. He also holds a Masters degree in Public Health from the University of Bedfordshire, United Kingdom.

He is the author of the poetry collection *Poetic Mirror.*